For Suesi and Richie

Text and illustrations © 1993 by Paul Dowling.
All rights reserved.
Printed in Malaysia.
First published 1993 by Orchard Books,
96 Leonard Street, London EC2A 4RH.
First published in the U.S. by Hyperion Books for Children,
114 Fifth Avenue, New York, New York 10011.

FIRST EDITION
1 3 5 7 9 10 8 6 4 2

Library of Congress Cataloging-in-Publication Data

Dowling, Paul
    You need a bath, Mustard/Paul Dowling—1st ed.
      p. cm.
    Summary: When he comes home all muddy, a bear's friends have fun
giving him a bath.
    ISBN 1–56282–392–2
    [1. Baths—Fiction.   2. Bears—Fiction.   3. Animals—Fiction.]
I. Title.
PZ7.D755Yp   1993
[E]—dc20   92–72933   CIP AC

The artwork for each picture is prepared with black pen and
colored inks.

You Need a Bath, Mustard

Paul Dowling

Hyperion Books for Children
New York

Puff, Rabbit, and Owl are following some muddy footprints.

Who could have made them?

Oh, Mustard. What have you been doing?

You need a bath.

Whoosh! Squirt! Lots of bubbles!

Your bath is ready, Mustard.

Splash! Not with your clothes on!

Scrub-a-dub-dub.

A bear in a tub.

Where is Mustard ?

Time to get dry.

Ooh! That tickles.

Whooooooooooooooo!

It's a ghost.

It's snowing!

A-a-a-a-choo!

Here is your bathrobe.

Here are your slippers.

A nice clean Mustard.

But where are Rabbit, Owl, and Puff?

They're all in the tub.

Hurray!